EMPOWERING TALES

SHORT STORIES FOR KIDS 9-12

CONTENTS PAGE

1. The Little Engine that Could: A Story of Perseverance

2. The Power of Kindness: A Story of Friendship

3. The Brave Little Mouse: A Story of Courage

4. The Starfish Story: A Story of Making a Difference

5. The Little Plant that Could: A Story of Growth

6. The Lost Kitten
7. The Brave Little Rabbit
8. The Magic Paint-brush
9. The Little Sparrow That could
10. The Little Match Girl
11. The Adventure of the Lost Kitten
12. The Secret Garden

1. The Little Engine that Could: A Story of Perseverance

Once upon a time, there was a little engine who lived on a train line. The other engines always laughed at him because he was small and not as strong as they were. They would tease him and call him names like "Tiny Tim" and "Little Larry". But the little engine never gave up. He knew that he could do anything if he just believed in himself.

One day, the big train that ran on the line broke down and the other engines were all busy. The train had to be pulled over a mountain and the other engines were too big and strong to do it. But the little engine, who had always been the smallest, stepped up to the challenge. The other engines laughed and said, "You can't do it, you're too small. The train is too heavy for you to pull." But the little engine believed in himself and said, "I think I can, I think I can."

The little engine started to pull the train, and at first, it was very hard. The train was heavy, and the mountain was steep. But the little engine kept going. He would say to himself, "I think I can, I think I can." The other engines were watching, and they couldn't believe it. They thought for sure that the little engine would give up, but he kept going.

The little engine pulled the train over the mountain and to the other side. The other engines were amazed and apologized for ever doubting him. From that day on, the little engine was known as the strongest engine on the line.

The little engine's determination and perseverance had paid off. He had shown that no matter how small or weak you may seem, you can accomplish great things if you just believe in yourself. He inspired the other engines to believe in themselves and never give up, no matter how hard the task may seem.

The little engine's story spread throughout the land, and people of all ages, came to hear it. Parents would tell it to their children, as a reminder of the power of perseverance. And the little engine became a legend, not just on the train line but in the hearts of many. He had shown that no matter how small or weak you may seem, you can accomplish great things if you just believe in yourself and never give up.

The little engine had proved that great things come in small packages, and with hard work, determination, and perseverance, you can achieve your dreams. He had inspired many and the story of the "The Little Engine that Could" became a classic, a story that would be passed down from generation to generation, as a reminder of the power of believing in oneself.

2.The Power of Kindness: A Story of Friendship

Once upon a time, there was a kind and friendly rabbit named Benny. Benny was well known throughout the forest for his generosity and willingness to help others. He would always go out of his way to help others, whether it was giving them a carrot from his garden or just a listening ear.

One day, a new rabbit named Jack moved into the forest. Jack was shy and didn't have any friends. He was new to the area and didn't know anyone. Benny noticed that Jack was feeling lonely and decided to take him under his wing. Benny welcomed Jack with open arms and showed him around the forest. He introduced Jack to all his friends and helped him to make new ones.

As they spent more time together, Benny and Jack became the best of friends. They went on adventures together and had a lot of fun. Jack was grateful to Benny for his kindness and friendship. He had never felt so welcomed and loved before.

Benny's kindness didn't just stop with Jack, he showed kindness to everyone he met. He would always be the first to help if someone needed it. His actions had a ripple effect, and the entire forest became a happier place. The animals in the forest began to follow Benny's example and started to show kindness to each other as well.

The forest was no longer a lonely place, it was a place of love and friendship. The animals would gather and have parties, and everyone was included. Even the most solitary animals would come out of their burrows to join in the fun.

The animals in the forest were so grateful to Benny for his kindness and friendship. They held a big party in his honor and presented him with a beautiful medal of honor. Benny was so touched by their kindness; he didn't know what to say. He was just glad that he could make a difference in their lives.

Benny's kindness had changed the forest forever, it was now a place of love and friendship. His actions had shown that one person can make a big difference in the world, and that kindness has the power to change lives. The story of Benny and his kindness spread throughout the land, and people of all ages, came to hear it. Parents would tell it to their children, as a reminder of the power of kindness and the impact of one person's actions on the world around them. Benny's kindness had not only changed the lives of the animals in the forest, but it had also touched the hearts of many.

3.The Brave Little Mouse: A Story of Courage

Once upon a time, there was a little mouse named Mia. Mia was small and timid, and she was always afraid of the big and fierce animals in the forest. She would always stay hidden in her burrow, not daring to venture out. But Mia had a big heart and a strong desire to help others.

One day, a group of hunters came to the forest and began trapping the animals. They set up traps everywhere and many animals were caught. The animals were afraid and didn't know what to do. They had never faced such danger before.

Mia knew she had to do something to save her friends. Despite her fear, she mustered up the courage to sneak into the hunter's camp and gnaw through the ropes that held the traps shut. She freed all the trapped animals and chased the hunters away.

The animals were amazed by Mia's bravery. They had never seen a mouse be so courageous before. From that day on, Mia was known as the bravest mouse in the forest. She had saved her friends and had shown that even the smallest and weakest of animals can make a big difference.

Mia's bravery had inspired the other animals in the forest. They realized that they didn't have to be afraid of the hunters anymore. They could stand up for themselves and protect their home. They formed a community watch, and they would work together to protect the forest from any danger.

The forest was now a safe place, and the animals were no longer afraid. They had learned that even the smallest and weakest of animals can make a big difference. They had learned that with courage and determination, anything is possible.

The story of Mia and her bravery spread throughout the land, and people of all ages, came to hear it. Parents would tell it to their children, as a reminder of the power of courage and determination. Mia's bravery had not only changed the lives of the animals in the forest, but it had also touched the hearts of many.

Mia's story had shown that no matter how small or weak you may seem, you can accomplish great things if you just believe in yourself and have the courage to stand up for what is right. It had shown that the smallest and weakest of creatures can make a big difference in the world, and that with courage and determination, anything is possible.

4. The Starfish Story: A Story of Making a Difference

Once upon a time, there was a young boy who loved to walk along the beach. He would spend hours walking along the shoreline, listening to the sound of the waves, and collecting shells. One day, as he was walking, he saw thousands of starfish that had washed up on the shore. They were dying because they couldn't get back to the water. The boy felt sad and helpless, but then he had an idea.

He started picking up one starfish at a time and throwing them back into the sea. A man walked by and saw what the boy was doing. He laughed and said, "You can't possibly make a difference. There are too many starfish and not enough of you." But the boy picked up another starfish and threw it back into the sea. "I made a difference to that one," he said. And with that, he continued to save as many starfish as he could.

The boy worked tirelessly, throwing starfish back into the sea, one by one. He didn't stop for hours. He didn't stop for food or water. He didn't stop for a break. He was determined to save as many starfish as he could.

As the day went on, more and more people started to notice the boy's efforts. They were inspired by his determination and started to help him. Soon, there were dozens of people on the beach, throwing starfish back into the sea. Together, they were able to save thousands of starfish.

The man who had laughed at the boy earlier, walked by once again. He saw the hundreds of people on the beach, working together to save the starfish. He felt ashamed of his earlier words and apologized to the boy. The boy smiled and said, "It's ok, it doesn't matter how many people join in, what matters is that we all made a difference to at least one starfish."

The boy's actions had shown that no matter how small or insignificant your actions may seem, you can make a difference. His actions had inspired many, and together, they had made a real difference in the lives of many starfish. His actions had shown that if everyone makes a small effort, together, we can achieve great things.

The story of the boy and the starfish spread throughout the land, and people of all ages, came to hear it. Parents would tell it to their children, as a reminder of the power of making a difference, no matter how small it may seem. The boy's actions had not only changed the lives of the starfish, but they had also touched the hearts of many and had inspired them to make a difference in their own way.

5. The Little Plant that Could: A Story of Growth

Once upon a time, there was a little seed that was planted in a garden. At first, it struggled to grow because it was small and weak. The other plants around it were bigger and stronger and they would often mock the little plant. They would say things like "You'll never grow into anything, you're too small" or "You'll never make it, you're not strong enough." But the little plant knew that it had the potential to grow into something great.

The little plant kept reaching for the sun and drinking up the water. It kept pushing through the soil, determined to grow. And slowly but surely, it started to grow. It grew taller and stronger, and soon, it had grown into a beautiful little plant. The other plants were amazed and apologized for ever doubting it.

The little plant continued to grow and soon it had grown into a beautiful flower. The flower had big petals, a bright and colorful center, and a sweet fragrance that filled the air. The other plants in the garden were in awe of its beauty and they were proud to have it as a part of their garden.

The little plant's growth had inspired the other plants in the garden. They realized that no matter how small or weak they may seem, they too had the potential to grow into something great. They realized that with hard work, determination and perseverance, anything is possible.

The little plant's story spread throughout the land, and people of all ages, came to hear it. Parents would tell it to their children, as a reminder of the power of growth and the importance of believing in oneself. The little plant had not only grown into a beautiful flower, but it had also touched the hearts of many and had inspired them to reach for their own potential and to never give up on their dreams.

The little plant's story showed that no matter how small or weak you may seem, you can accomplish great things if you just believe in yourself and never give up. It showed that with hard work, determination, and perseverance, you can reach your potential and become something beautiful. It was a reminder that everyone has the potential to grow, and that we should never give up on ourselves, or on our dreams.

6. The Lost Kitten

Once upon a time, there was a little kitten named Mittens. She was a playful and curious kitten, always getting into mischief. Her owners loved her dearly, but they couldn't help but worry about her safety. Mittens had a habit of wandering off, and every time she did, she would come back with a new scratch or bruise.

One day, Mittens decided to explore the forest behind her house. It was a place she had never been before, and the tall trees and rustling leaves called out to her. She pranced through the underbrush, chasing butterflies and birds. She climbed over logs and splashed through streams. She was having the time of her life.

But as the sun began to set, Mittens realized that she had been gone for a long time. She looked around and saw that she was in an unfamiliar place. She couldn't see her house, and she couldn't hear the sound of her family. She was lost.

At first, Mittens wasn't too worried. She figured she would just follow her nose and she would eventually find her way back home. But as she walked, the forest seemed to change. The trees grew taller and thicker, blocking out the sun. The ground became muddier, and the air grew colder. Mittens grew tired and hungry. She meowed for her family, but there was no answer.

Mittens sat down and cried. She was lost, and she was alone. She missed her family and her warm bed. She wished she had never left home.

Just when she thought things couldn't get any worse, it started to rain. The drops pelted her fur and soaked through to her skin. Mittens shivered and huddled under a bush, trying to stay dry. She was cold, wet, and miserable.

But then she remembered something her mother had told her. "If you ever get lost, look for the tallest tree and follow it. It will lead you home." Mittens looked around and saw a towering pine tree in the distance. She stood up and started to walk towards it. It was a long and difficult journey, but Mittens kept going. She climbed over fallen logs and splashed through puddles. She meowed for her family, but there was still no answer.

Finally, she reached the tree. She looked up and saw the sky through the branches. She meowed one last time and heard a faint meow in return. She looked down and saw her house in the distance. She had done it, she had found her way home.

Mittens ran as fast as she could, her paws pounding the ground. She burst through the door and into the arms of her family. They were overjoyed to see her and hugged her tightly. They were worried sick and thought they had lost her. Mittens was happy to be back home, safe and sound.

From that day on, Mittens never wandered too far from home. She had learned her lesson and knew how important it was to be safe. But she never forgot the tall pine tree that had led her home, and she always remembered the love of her family

7. The Brave little Rabbit

Once upon a time, there was a little rabbit named Peter. He was always afraid of everything, and he never wanted to leave his burrow. His brothers and sisters were always out exploring and having adventures, but Peter was content to stay at home. He was afraid of the forest, the meadow, and even the garden. He was afraid of the birds, the bees, and even the butterflies. He was just afraid of everything.

One day, Peter heard that a farmer was coming to take all the carrots in the field. The other animals were worried and didn't know what to do. They had heard that the farmer was very mean and that he would take all the carrots, leaving nothing for the animals. They were worried that they would starve.

Peter felt a sudden urge to do something. He realized that he had always been afraid, but he didn't want to be afraid anymore. He wanted to be brave like his brothers and sisters. He wanted to help the other animals.

He hopped out of his burrow and started to make his way to the field. He was scared, but he kept going. He hopped over rocks and through the tall grass. He hopped past the birds and the bees, and even the butterflies. He was determined to make it to the field.

When he finally got there, he saw the farmer's truck parked in the middle of the field. The farmer was already digging up the carrots and putting them in the truck. Peter hopped up to the truck and stood in front of it. The farmer was surprised to see such a little rabbit being so brave.

"What do you want, little rabbit?" the farmer asked.

"I want you to stop taking the carrots," Peter said. "The carrots belong to all the animals in the forest, and we need them to survive."

The farmer looked at Peter and saw the determination in his eyes. He saw that Peter was not just a scared little rabbit, but a brave one.

"You're right," the farmer said. "I shouldn't take the carrots. I'll leave them for the animals."

The farmer got back in his truck and drove away. Peter watched as the truck disappeared into the distance. He had done it. He had stood up for what was right, and he had helped the other animals.

Peter hopped back to his burrow, feeling proud of himself. His brothers and sisters were amazed at what he had done. They had always thought that Peter was too scared to do anything, but he had proved them wrong.

From that day on, Peter was not afraid anymore. He had learned that being brave doesn't mean you're not afraid, it just means you do what's right even when you are. And he had also learned that sometimes, the smallest and seemingly weakest creatures can make the biggest impact. He went on to have many more adventures and helped out his community in many ways. He was loved and respected by all, and he lived a life filled with courage and kindness.

8.The Magic Paintbrush

Once upon a time, there was a poor boy named Ming. He loved to draw and he would spend hours sketching and painting. He would draw the houses in his village, the animals in the forest, and the stars in the sky. He would draw anything and everything that caught his eye.

One day, a kind old man came to Ming's village. He saw Ming sitting by the side of the road, drawing. The old man asked Ming what he was drawing, and Ming showed him his sketchbook. The old man was impressed by Ming's talent and he asked Ming if he would like a gift. Ming was surprised, but he said yes.

The old man gave Ming a paintbrush, and he said that it was a magic paintbrush. He told Ming that if he painted something with this brush, it would come to life. Ming was amazed, he had never heard of such a thing. He thanked the old man and went back home to try it out.

Ming's mother was sick and he decided to paint a beautiful garden for her. He drew a garden with a pond, a waterfall, and a rainbow. He used the magic paintbrush and as he painted, the garden came to life. His mother was so happy to see the garden and she felt instantly cured. She hugged Ming and thanked him for the beautiful garden.

Ming wanted to share the magic of the paintbrush with others, so he went to the village square and painted a feast for the poor. He drew a table with a roast turkey, a pot of soup, and a bowl of fruit. He used the magic paintbrush and as he painted, the feast came to life. The poor villagers were so grateful and they thanked Ming for the delicious food.

Ming then decided to paint a playground for the children of the village. He drew a playground with swings, a slide and a seesaw. He used the magic paintbrush and as he painted, the playground came to life. The children were so excited and they thanked Ming for the wonderful playground.

Ming was happy, he had used the magic paintbrush to make the world a better place. But one day, the old man came back to take the paintbrush back, saying that it was only lent to him. Ming was sad, but the old man told him that he had taught Ming how to make the world a better place, and that was the true magic of the paintbrush. Ming understood, he knew that he didn't need the paintbrush to make a difference in the world, he just needed to have a kind heart and a creative mind.

He continued to paint and draw, and his art brought joy to many people. He became known as the "Magician of the Brush" and people came from far and wide to see his work. He lived a long and fulfilling life, and his legacy lived on through his art.

The magic paintbrush had not just brought his drawings to life, it had brought Ming's kindness and generosity to life, and that was the greatest magic of all.

9. The Little Sparrow That could

Once upon a time, there was a poor boy named Ming. He loved to draw and he would spend hours sketching and painting. He would draw the houses in his village, the animals in the forest, and the stars in the sky. He would draw anything and everything that caught his eye.

One day, a kind old man came to Ming's village. He saw Ming sitting by the side of the road, drawing. The old man asked Ming what he was drawing, and Ming showed him his sketchbook. The old man was impressed by Ming's talent and he asked Ming if he would like a gift. Ming was surprised, but he said yes.

The old man gave Ming a paintbrush, and he said that it was a magic paintbrush. He told Ming that if he painted something with this brush, it would come to life. Ming was amazed, he had never heard of such a thing. He thanked the old man and went back home to try it out.

Ming's mother was sick and he decided to paint a beautiful garden for her. He drew a garden with a pond, a waterfall, and a rainbow. He used the magic paintbrush and as he painted, the garden came to life. His mother was so happy to see the garden and she felt instantly cured. She hugged Ming and thanked him for the beautiful garden.

Ming wanted to share the magic of the paintbrush with others, so he went to the village square and painted a feast for the poor. He drew a table with a roast turkey, a pot of soup, and a bowl of fruit. He used the magic paintbrush and as he painted, the feast came to life. The poor villagers were so grateful and they thanked Ming for the delicious food.

Ming then decided to paint a playground for the children of the village. He drew a playground with swings, a slide and a see-saw. He used the magic paintbrush and as he painted, the playground came to life. The children were so excited and they thanked Ming for the wonderful playground.

Ming was happy, he had used the magic paintbrush to make the world a better place. But one day, the old man came back to take the paintbrush back, saying that it was only lent to him. Ming was sad, but the old man told him that he had taught Ming how to make the world a better place, and that was the true magic of the paintbrush. Ming understood, he knew that he didn't need the paintbrush to make a difference in the world, he just needed to have a kind heart and a creative mind.

He continued to paint and draw, and his art brought joy to many people. He became known as the "Magician of the Brush" and people came from far and wide to see his work. He lived a long and fulfilling life, and his legacy lived on through his art.

The magic paintbrush had not just brought his drawings to life, it had brought Ming's kindness and generosity to life, and that was the greatest magic of all.

10. The Little Match Girl

Once upon a time, there was a poor girl named Mary. Mary lived in a small village, and she had very little. She didn't have a warm home, clothes, or even enough food to eat. Despite her hardships, Mary never lost hope. She would always look for the good in everything and would always find a way to smile.

One day, Mary saw a shooting star in the sky, and she made a wish. She wished that she could have a beautiful Christmas, with a warm home, clothes, and food to eat. The next day, a kind old lady came to the village and saw Mary's plight. She took pity on her and offered her a place to stay, warm clothes, and food to eat.

On Christmas Eve, the kind old lady invited Mary to her home. She decorated her home with beautiful ornaments and had a big Christmas tree. They had a big feast with delicious food, and the kind old lady even gave Mary a beautiful dress. Mary was so happy, and she couldn't believe that her wish had come true.

The kind old lady was none other than an angel in disguise, who was sent to help Mary. Mary's kindness and determination had touched the hearts of many, even the heavens. Her story spread throughout the village, and people were touched by her kindness and determination. They realized that no matter how poor or hard life may seem, there is always hope and a way to be happy.

From that day on, Mary's Christmas wish became a tradition in the village, and every Christmas, the villagers would gather together and help the poor and less fortunate. Mary's kindness and determination had not only changed her own life, but it had also changed the lives of many in the village. Parents would tell her story to their children, as a reminder of the power of hope, kindness and determination. Mary's story had shown that no matter how hard life may seem, there is always a way to be happy and to make a difference in the world.

11. The Adventure of the Lost Kitten

Once upon a time, in a small village, there lived a little girl named Emily. One day, while playing outside, Emily's kitten, Whiskers, got lost. Emily was heartbroken and didn't know what to do. She asked her friends and family to help her look for Whiskers, but no one had seen him.

Feeling hopeless, Emily decided to take matters into her own hands. She put on her favorite pink dress and her trusty red backpack, and set off into the woods to search for her kitten.

As she walked deeper into the woods, she heard a faint meowing sound. She followed the sound and soon came across a cave. Inside, she found Whiskers, who had gotten trapped by a pile of rocks. Emily quickly freed her kitten and they hugged each other tightly.

As they were about to leave the cave, Emily noticed a sparkly object on the cave floor. She picked it up and found that it was a beautiful diamond! Emily knew that the diamond belonged to the king, who had lost it while on a walk. She hurriedly went to the king's palace and returned the diamond, who was very happy and grateful. In return, the king offered a reward to Emily and Whiskers, who had become the best of friends.

12.The Secret Garden

Once upon a time, in a far-off land, there was a grand castle that had been abandoned for many years. The castle was surrounded by a lush, overgrown garden that had been untouched for just as long. The villagers whispered stories of a secret garden hidden within the castle walls, but no one had ever been able to find it.

One day, a young girl named Rose moved to the village with her family. She was a curious and adventurous girl, and she couldn't resist the pull of the mysterious garden. Every day, she would explore the castle grounds, searching for the secret garden.

One afternoon, as she was wandering through the castle, she heard a faint whispering coming from behind a large stone wall. Intrigued, she followed the sound and soon found a small, hidden door. Without hesitation, Rose opened the door and stepped inside.

The secret garden was more beautiful than she could have ever imagined. The sun shone down through the trees, dappling the ground with light. Flowers of every color bloomed, and the air was filled with the sweet scent of blooming roses.

As Rose explored the garden, she met a group of friendly fairies who lived there. They were delighted to meet her and showed her all the wonders of the secret garden. They showed her a special fountain that had the power to grant wishes and a magical tree that would grant you a wish if you could climb to the top. Rose was amazed by all the beauty and magic of the secret garden.

As the days passed, Rose visited the secret garden more and more often. She would spend hours exploring and playing with the fairies. She would tell them all about her adventures in the village and her family. The fairies became her best friends, and she felt like she had found her true home in the secret garden.

But one day, as Rose was returning to the village, she was confronted by a group of thieves who had heard of the secret garden and its magical powers. They demanded that Rose show them the way to the garden, but she refused. She knew that the garden belonged to the fairies and that it was not for humans to exploit.

Determined to protect her friends and their home, Rose rallied the villagers to her cause. Together, they fought off the thieves and protected the secret garden.

From that day on, Rose was known as the protector of the secret garden. She would visit the garden often, and she and the fairies would go on many more adventures together. The secret garden remained a place of magic and wonder, known only to a select few. And Rose knew that as long as she was there, the garden would always be safe.

www.ingramcontent.com/pod-product-compliance
Lightning Source LLC
LaVergne TN
LVHW080040170826
845677LV00025B/1926

* 9 7 9 8 3 7 4 8 8 9 9 0 1 *